CHUM

comixtribe.com

CHUM
First Printing. January 2017
ISBN: 978-0-9967724-4-0

PRINTED IN USA.

CHUM

SAMI KIVELA · RYAN K LINDSAY
ARTIST · CO-CREATORS · WRITER

MARK DALE · COLORIST

NIC J SHAW · LETTERER

DAN HILL · EDITOR

CHAPTER ONE

KINGSFORD ISLAND. IN THE MIDDLE OF THE ANNUAL BOMBORA SURF COMPETITION.

AT THE START OF ONE HELL OF A STORM.

SUMMER LOVED THE STORMS ON KINGSFORD ISLAND. THEY ALWAYS FELT UNCERTAIN AND DANGEROUS. THEY WERE FUN.

SHE WAS THAT PERFECT WAVE YOU'D WAIT ALL DAY FOR.

PENNY LOVED THE PEOPLE OF KINGSFORD ISLAND. THEY NEVER CHALLENGED HIM. THEY OFTEN RELIED UPON HIM.

HE WAS THE SILENT UNDERTOW THAT WAITED FOR EVERYONE.

STANDARD HATED EVERYTHING ABOUT KINGSFORD ISLAND. THERE WAS TOO MUCH SAND, NOT MUCH TO DO, AND STRANGELY ENOUGH NO DARK BEER.

HE WAS THE OAR THAT CHURNED AND SHAPED THE WATER.

BOMBORA BROUGHT EVERYONE ON KINGSFORD TOGETHER. IT MEANT A LOT TO THE PEOPLE ON THE SHORE...

NOT JOINING THEM OUT THERE, PENNY?

NAH, NOT A GOOD DAY FOR IT. THERE'LL BE BLOOD IN THIS WATER.

BUT YOU STILL WANTED TO TURN UP AND SEE IT?

BUSINESS IS BUSINESS.

YOU PAYING FOR THAT?

YOU WANNA TAKE EVEN MORE?

=SIGH=

WHY ARE YOU HERE?

THE FREE BEER.

YOU KNOW MY CUSTOMERS GET ITCHY WITH A BADGE IN THE ROOM. AND DESPITE LIVING ON A BEACH, YOU LOATHE SURFING. *WHY* ARE YOU HERE?

MIGHT AS WELL WATCH SOMETHING WHILE I GET DRUNK.

I SHOULD AT LEAST KNOW IF SOMETHING IS GOING TO HAPPEN.

WHY D'YOU THINK PENNY'S HERE? HE RARELY SLUMS IT WITH US PLEBS. I KNOW HIS CUSTOMERS ARE SURFERS, BUT HE ISN'T.

I CAN'T SURF EITHER, BUT I RUN THIS SHACK LIKE I'M HALF MERMAID. YOU CAN'T BLAME THE MAN FOR EVERY LITTLE THING.

YOU KNOW WHAT'S FUNNY? I PROBABLY COULD BLAME HIM FOR EVERY LITTLE THING AND I'D BE RIGHT. THE GUY IS BAD NEWS.

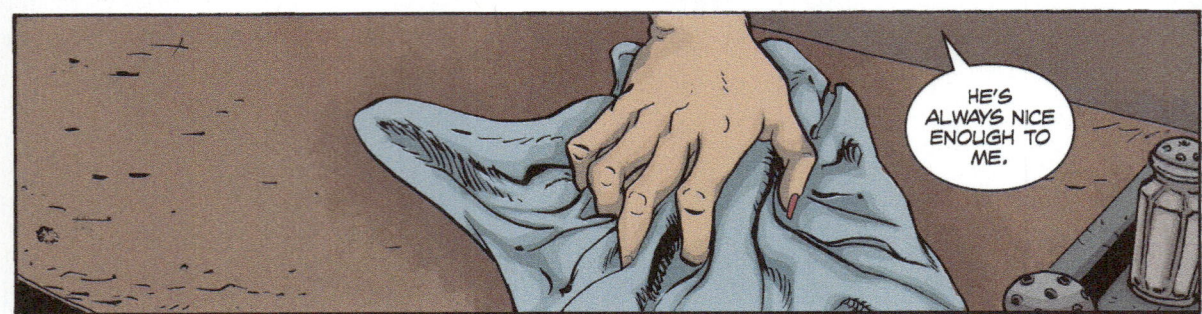

HE'S ALWAYS NICE ENOUGH TO ME.

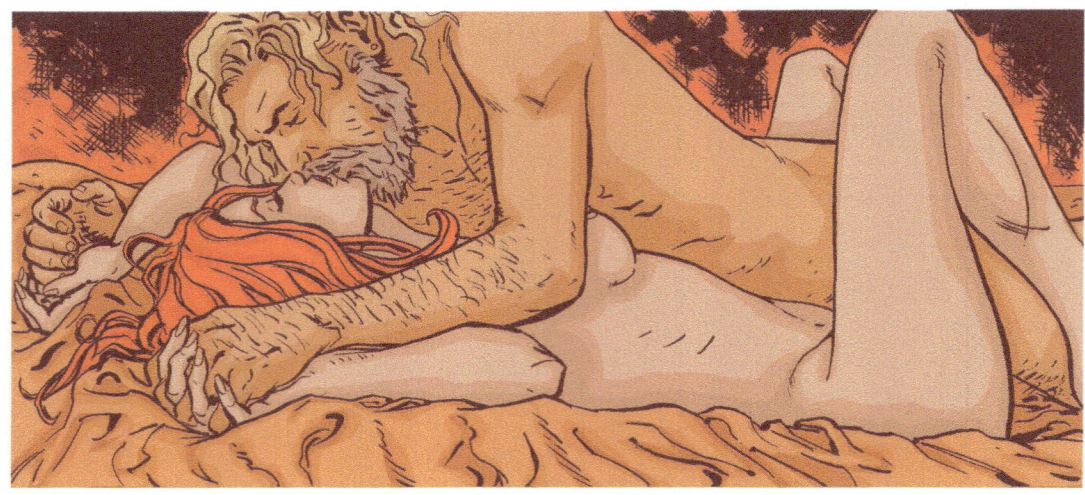

THEN YOU'RE BLIND. AND STUPID. PENNY IS NO NICE GUY...

"...HE'S THE SPARK THAT'S GOING TO BURN THIS ISLAND DOWN."

THOCK

KINGSFORD ISLAND WAS A PLACE OF VIOLENCE. AND ALL WERE TO BLAME FOR THIS.

GROWING UP HERE, MAN, IT WAS PARADISE. NOW, IT'S PURGATORY.

PEOPLE HERE EITHER WAITING TO DIE OR TO MOVE ON TO SOMETHING ELSE.

I KNOW WHICH ONE I AM.

BUT WHILE I'M STUCK HERE, I FEEL BETTER KNOWING THERE'S A WHITE KNIGHT AROUND.

THE NIGHT BECOMES A BLUR, BUT SHE REMAINS IN FOCUS.

"HE CAN SLEEP IT OFF ON MY COUCH.

"AFTER LETTING YOU ASSHOLES DO HIM LIKE THIS, THE LEAST I CAN DO FOR HIM IS BREAKFAST.

"SLEEP.

"LET ME PROTECT YOU FOR JUST ONE NIGHT."

HIS STOMACH IS
A WASTELAND.

BUT IF
HE'S HONEST WITH
HIMSELF, HE'S NOT
FRONTING FOR THE
BACON AND EGGS.

MORNING, GUS.
BREAKFAST?

EXTRA MUSHROOMS.
BUTTER LIKE YOU'RE
DROWNING
'EM.

NO
PROBLEM.

A MENU
IN CASE
YOU WANT
A DRINK.

GUS READS THE
NOTE QUIETLY.

The man in the booth is waiting for you to leave.

He comes in every Monday morning,

bringing the same trouble.

I don't know what to do about it,

but everything will be normal after he leaves.

Just wait it out.

YOU WANT AN AUTOGRAPH, IT'S GONNA COST YOU, SON.

IN GUS' DEFENSE, HE WASN'T JUST HUNGOVER, HE WAS STILL DRUNK.

THIS WAS YEARS OF SILENT PINING FINALLY MAKING A NOISE.

GUS WALTERS WAS UNDER TOO MANY INFLUENCES THIS MORNING.

FUCK OFF.

ISN'T THIS WHAT YOU WANTED?

SWAMPY IS DEAD.

THANK YOU.

SUMMER IS THINKING VERY QUICKLY ON HER FEET.

CLEAN THE TABLE, GET RID OF EVERYTHING.

HOW BIG IS YOUR FREEZER?

GUS IS DRUNK ENOUGH TO BELIEVE THIS IS ALL GOING TO WORK.

MEN ARE SUCKERS FOR REDHEADS AND GREENBACKS.

HOLY SHIT.

THERE'S ENOUGH CASH AND DRUGS HERE TO RETIRE ON.

WE COULD LEAVE HERE, THIS SHIT, START A NEW LIFE.

NO MORE PENNY, NO MORE LIVING WEEK TO WEEK.

I CAN LOOK AFTER YOU. WE...

WE CAN BE HAPPY. ISN'T THIS WHAT YOU WANT?

GUS WENT OUT ABOUT TWO HOURS AGO NOW. I WATCHED BECAUSE IF HE NAILED ONE OF THOSE BIG WAVES OUT BACK IT WAS GOING TO BE SLICK.

I LOST SIGHT OF HIM, THEN HIS BOARD CAME BACK ALONE.

THANKS FOR YOUR TIME. WE'LL BE IN TOUCH.

YOU THINK IT'S AS SIMPLE AS IT SOUNDS?

GUS PROBABLY GOT EATEN BY SHARKS OUT THERE, DOES THAT SOUND SIMPLE TO YOU?

OR IS IT ACTUALLY EASIER FOR YOUR VICTIM TO DISAPPEAR? SAVE YOU FROM THE WORK?

IT SOUNDS CONVENIENT.

SO IT'S GOING TO BE ANOTHER ONE OF THOSE PIECES?

IF YOU MEAN WHERE I INVESTIGATE YOUR DRUNKEN INEPTITUDE AND ABILITY TO MAKE THE ISLAND A WORSE PLACE...

ABSOLUTELY.

PENNY'S MAN ATTACKS GUS AND THEN GUS INEXPLICABLY DISAPPEARS.

SOLVE THIS ONE AND YOU HAVE MY RESPECT.

WHO SAYS I NEED THAT?

PLEASE, WHAT ELSE HAVE YOU GOT TO WORK FOR?

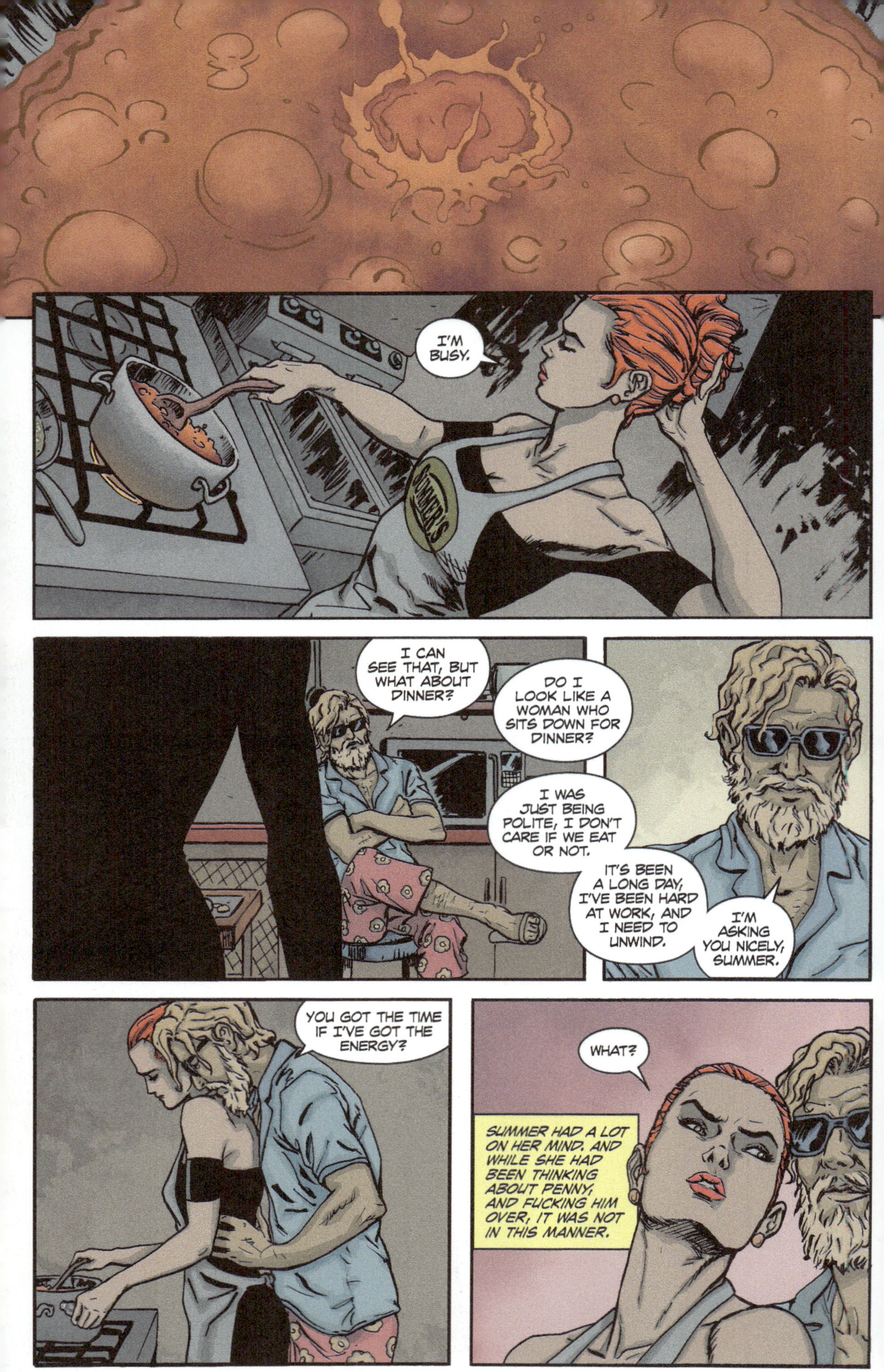

I'M BUSY.

I CAN SEE THAT, BUT WHAT ABOUT DINNER?

DO I LOOK LIKE A WOMAN WHO SITS DOWN FOR DINNER?

I WAS JUST BEING POLITE, I DON'T CARE IF WE EAT OR NOT.

IT'S BEEN A LONG DAY; I'VE BEEN HARD AT WORK, AND I NEED TO UNWIND.

I'M ASKING YOU NICELY, SUMMER.

YOU GOT THE TIME IF I'VE GOT THE ENERGY?

WHAT?

SUMMER HAD A LOT ON HER MIND, AND WHILE SHE HAD BEEN THINKING ABOUT PENNY, AND FUCKING HIM OVER, IT WAS NOT IN THIS MANNER.

YOU'RE A REAL CLASS ACT, OFFICER.

WHAT THE FUCK WAS HE DOING HERE?

CONSPIRING WITH ME TO KILL YOU SO WE COULD GET YOUR DIAMOND MINE BEFORE OUR DIVORCE KICKS IN.

YOU TWO BETTER ACT FAST BECAUSE AS SOON AS YOU SIGN THESE I'M A FREE AGENT.

PETITION FOR DIVORCE

I'LL GET TO THESE LATER, I'M BUSY NOW.

SERIOUSLY, WHY WAS HE HERE? ARE YOU IN TROUBLE?

NOTHING I'M NOT HANDLING.

EXCUSE ME? HELLO-OO?

GOD, YOU AGAIN.

YOU'LL BE HAPPY TO KNOW I'M NOT HERE FOR YOU.

HAVE YOU SEEN SWAMPY?

WHY?

LIKE I SAID, I'M NOT HERE FOR YOU.

HE'S MISSING, A FEW DAYS. THEY SAY HE CAME HERE A LOT. I'M PIECING THE STORY TOGETHER.

SOMEONE HAS TO.

NO, LAST I SAW HIM WAS ABOUT A WEEK AGO.

HE GOT EGGS, COFFEE, THE USUAL.

STANDARD HAD A SERIES OF TELLS. IT TOOK SUMMER ABOUT 5 MONTHS TO LEARN THEM ALL.

I'D LOVE TO TALK ABOUT THEORETICAL CRIMES BETWEEN DEADBEATS, BUT I'VE GOT WORK TO DO.

YOU CALL IT WORK BUT YOU MAKE BEING CLOWN SHOES LOOK LIKE CHILD'S PLAY.

YEP, GO FUCK YOURSELF.

HOW OFTEN DID SWAMPY COME IN HERE?

...Y'KNOW, STANDARD'S HUNG LIKE A ROGUE ELEPHANT. FLIRT ALL YOU WANT, YOU COULDN'T TAKE IT.

...

SUMMER DOESN'T KNOW WHAT THE CONNECTION IS BUT SHE FEELS IT IN THE AIR, TAUT, LIKE PIANO WIRE AROUND HER THROAT.

BECAUSE SHE KNOWS THAT LOOK IN STANDARD'S EYES. SHE KNOWS SHE'S FUCKED UP SOMEHOW.

PLEASE, NO.

AND SHE KNOWS EVERYTHING IS BROKEN.

BUT THERE ARE A LOT OF THINGS YOU CAN DO WITH BROKEN SHARDS.

NO, NO, NO.

C'MON, SWAMPY, PICK UP, YOU PRICK...

TINGA-LA TINGA-LA

TINGA-LA TINGA-LA

...FUUUU-CK.

CHAPTER TWO

BOBBY LEVEL, CHRIST, THERE'S A NAME I HAVEN'T THOUGHT ABOUT IN YEARS.

THAT CHEATING LITTLE DICK.

Y'KNOW, I STITCHED HIM UP. I KISSED HIM AT THAT PARTY, THE ONE ON THE BOAT.

YEAH, THE ONE WITH THE CAGES.

THEN I ASKED IF HE COULD TASTE GARRY'S CUM.

I WAS SUCH A BITCH.

NO, I DIDN'T BLOW GARRY. YOU DID, A MONTH EARLIER, YOU DIRTY WHORE.

I'M NOT SURPRISED YOU HEARD ABOUT IT, WHY'D YOU NEVER ASK ME?

NO, I DIDN'T, BECAUSE WHO CARES WHAT THOSE ASSHOLES THINK?

I AM WHAT I AM, NEVER WHAT THEY THINK I AM.

JOHN MARSH WAS A GUY STANDARD KNEW IN TRAINING.

A WORLD AWAY NOW.

OR IS THIS--THIS RIGHT HERE AND NOW--THE FOREIGN LAND?

ABOUT THE ONLY THING STANDARD EVER MANAGED TO GET DONE ON THE ISLAND WAS PUT MARSH IN PENNY'S CREW AS DEEP COVER.

DO YOU WANT TO TELL ME NOW HOW YOU'RE GOING TO BOTCH THIS ONE OR DO YOU THINK I ENJOY THE ANTICIPATION?

I THINK I'M LOSING MY MIND.

I'M NOT KIDDING. I THINK THERE'S IRREPARABLE CEREBRAL DAMAGE.

THEN LET'S SWITCH YOUR MIND OFF.

MAYBE YOUR MOUTH MIGHT FOLLOW.

SUMMER DIDN'T LOVE PENNY. SOMETIMES SHE DOWNRIGHT LOATHED HIM. BUT SHE BELIEVED THAT YOU TOOK A FUCK BUDDY FOR A REASON OR A SEASON. PENNY WAS BOTH.

HE WAS A FANTASTIC LAY, AND HE WAS MERELY AN ARROW IN A QUIVER.

ALL FOR ONE FINAL FRESH START.

BUT FOR SOMETHING TO BEGIN...

...ANOTHER THING MUST END.

WHERE ARE WE GOING?

US? NOWHERE.

THAT SOUNDS OMINOUS.

WHERE DO WE HAVE TO BE? IF WE DON'T GO ANYWHERE THEN WE'LL ALWAYS BE LIKE THIS, THIS HAPPY, THIS LUCKY.

BESIDES, THIS IS THE ISLAND, WHERE COULD WE GO? AND WHERE ELSE WOULD WE WANT TO BE?

G'NIGHT, PENNY, SWEET DREAMS.

SO, WHERE ARE WE GOING?

GAH!

GUS HAS KILLED A MAN, HIDDEN A FORTUNE IN MONEY AND DRUGS, FAKED HIS OWN DEATH, SWAM AROUND THE ISLAND, AND NOW FOUND IT WAS ALL FOR NAUGHT.

HE SPENT HIS TIME HIDING AND HOPING. THE PLAN TO WAIT, COLLECT SUMMER AND THEIR GOODS, AND LEAVE THE ISLAND WAS SO SIMPLE IT HAD TO WORK.

BUT THERE WAS NO REASON TO BELIEVE SUMMER WOULD EVER FEEL ANYTHING FOR HIM EXCEPT THAT HE WANTED IT SO DAMN MUCH.

GUS FEELS LIKE AN IDIOT.

SUMMER DOESN'T FEEL MUCH OF ANYTHING AT ALL.

STANDARD KNEW WHEN HE MET SUMMER HE'D DO ANYTHING FOR HER. IT'S WHY HE LOVED HER SO MUCH AND WHY HE WENT ON TO HATE HER WITH EQUAL PASSION.

BUT LOVE OR HATE, IT NEVER STOPPED IT BEING TRUE.

SLAP

WHETHER HE WANTED TO OR NOT, WHETHER HE REALISED IT OR NOT, HE ALWAYS ENDED UP DOING WHATEVER SHE NEEDED.

SUMMER'S SUPERPOWER WAS THE ABILITY TO GET SHIT DONE.

HANNAH KEPT A FILE ON ANYONE OF ANY IMPORTANCE ON KINGSFORD ISLAND. SOME OF THE UNIMPORTANT PEOPLE, TOO.

IT WAS A MIXTURE OF BEING BORED AND THE FACT THE ISLAND HOUSED A CORNUCOPIA OF SCUM AND THIEVES.

GIGANTIC ASSHOLES LIKE PENNY STOOD OUT FROM THE PACK, BUT THEY WERE LOW HANGING FRUIT AS FAR AS STORIES GO.

BESIDES, HALF THE ISLAND EITHER WORKED FOR PENNY OR RELIED ON HIS TRADE.

HANNAH EVEN CURATED A FILE ON HERSELF. SHE KEPT IT IN HER BEDSIDE TABLE.

IT WASN'T FOR THE AUTOBIOGRAPHY SHE HOPED SHE'D HAVE REASON TO WRITE ONE DAY. SHE KEPT THE FILE IN CASE ANYTHING EVER HAPPENED TO HER.

HANNAH WAS COLLECTING THE THREADS TO THE UNOFFICIAL HISTORY OF KINGSFORD ISLAND BUT ONE PERSON SHE HAD LITTLE TO NOTHING ON WAS...

GUS' BOARDS

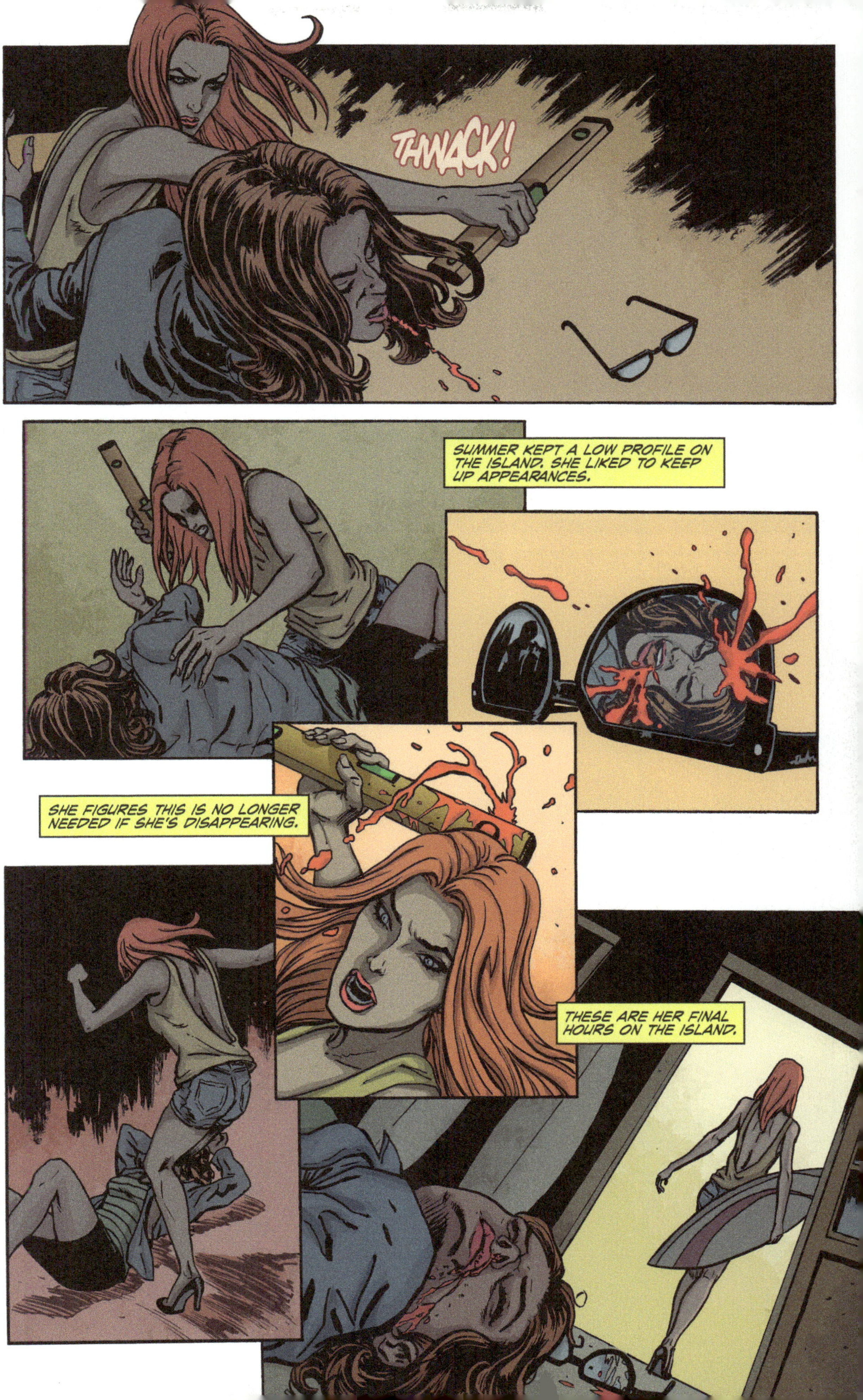

THWACK!

SUMMER KEPT A LOW PROFILE ON THE ISLAND. SHE LIKED TO KEEP UP APPEARANCES.

SHE FIGURES THIS IS NO LONGER NEEDED IF SHE'S DISAPPEARING.

THESE ARE HER FINAL HOURS ON THE ISLAND.

STANDARD CAME TO KINGSFORD ISLAND BECAUSE OF SUMMER.

HER FATHER DIED, SHE GOT THE BUSINESS, IT WAS A PLACE TO BE. HELL, IT EVEN GOT TO BE FUN AT TIMES.

BUT IT WAS ONLY SUPPOSED TO BE FOR A FEW YEARS.

THEY'D LEAVE ONCE THEY WERE EXPECTING, THEY TOLD THEMSELVES.

BUT ALL THEY COULD EXPECT WAS HEARTBREAK.

THEY WEREN'T GOING TO LEAVE AS THREE. AND THE MORE STANDARD DRANK THE CLOSER HE CAME TO LEAVING AS ONE.

THERE WAS A TIME WHERE STANDARD LOVED SUMMER MORE THAN THE MOON AND THE STARS. BUT THAT WAS ALL SUNK BENEATH THE WAVES NOW.

OVER TIME, STANDARD CAME TO LOATHE SUMMER. SHE REMINDED HIM OF HIS FAILURE, ALL HE COULD NOT BRING HER. HE BECAME BITTER AND SHE BECAME BROKEN.

HE COULD HAVE LEFT ANY TIME, BUT WHERE WOULD HE GO, AND WHO WOULD HAVE HIM?

PART OF HIM STUCK AROUND TO PROVE HE COULD RESIST HER. HE FELT POWER IN THAT.

BUT ON THIS NIGHT, FINALLY, HE NEEDED TO LEAVE THE ISLAND. SOMETHING SHE WOULD NEVER DO, SOMETHING HE ALWAYS SHOULD HAVE DONE.

IT WOULD INDEED BE A GOOD BYE.

HELLLLL--

--OH!

JESUS, WHAT'RE YOU DOING HERE?

PICKING UP THE PAPERS.

OH.

...CAN I COME IN?

...

C'MON, I GOTTA PISS.

SUMMER HAD DELAYED THE DIVORCE, THROUGH VARIOUS MEANS, FOR HALF A YEAR. SHE DIDN'T EVEN KNOW WHY.

I DON'T WANT TO BE RUDE--

HA!

--BUT CAN WE DO THIS QUICK? I'VE GOT THINGS TO GET ON WITH.

FLUSH

YOU'VE GOT THINGS TO GET ON WITH? JESUS.

I NEVER FIT IN HERE.

YOU EVER WONDER WHY I STAYED?

THIS IS YOUR ISLAND, AND I HAD EVERY REASON TO LEAVE, AND YET I STAYED. Y'KNOW WHY?

I THINK I DID IT BECAUSE I KNEW IT'D MAKE ME MISERABLE.

I TOLD MYSELF PLENTY OF OTHER BULLSHIT TO DISTRACT FROM THE CLOCK MOVING BUT IN THE END I'VE BEEN PUNISHING MYSELF FOR SOMETHING THAT WASN'T MY FAULT.

KNOWING THAT, FINALLY, I THINK I'M READY TO LEAVE.

CLICK

WHAT?

I DIDN'T KNOW HE WAS WITH YOU, SWAMPY.

HE WAS UNDERCOVER, YEAH?

WE WENT AFTER HIM. I KNEW HE RAN THE MONEY. BUT THIS ISN'T...

THIS ISN'T ABOUT US.

IT'S JUST AN ACCIDENT.

YOU KILL AN INNOCENT MAN. A GOOD MAN.

I'M SORRY.

SORRY ISN'T GOING TO BRING HIM BACK.

THE APOLOGY'S NOT FOR WHAT I'VE DONE...

IT'S ALWAYS THE SAME. YOU LET A GIRL LIKE SUMMER TOO CLOSE...

CHAPTER THREE

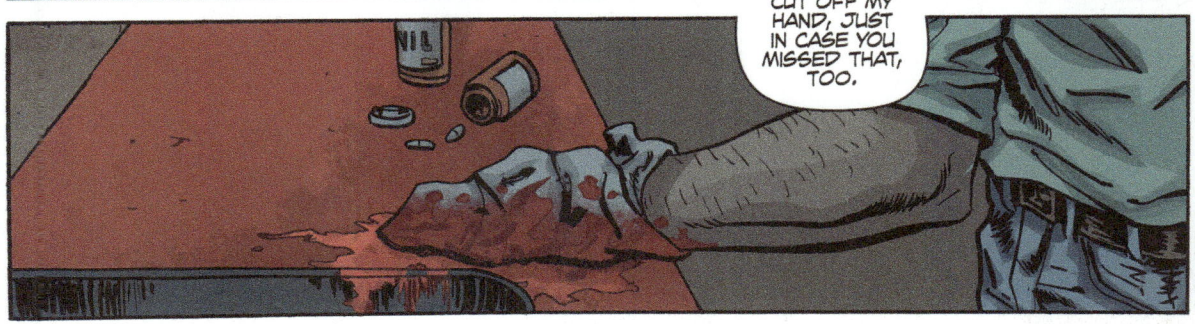

MAYBE YOU SHOULD TELL ME EVERYTHING THAT HAPPENED, SLOWLY AND IN DETAIL, BEFORE YOU DIE.

RELAX, I'M NOT DYING. BULLET PASSED THROUGH CLEAN.

YOU CAN STILL DIE FRO--

LISTEN, I GOT TAMPONS STUFFED INSIDE MY CHEST, MY EYESIGHT IS BLURRING FROM PAIN, AND I DON'T KNOW WHERE THE HELL SHE PUT MY HAND.

SHE'S GONE, STANDARD. GONE.

IT WAS ALWAYS A WAR OF ATTRITION WITH SUMMER.

I SHOULD HAVE WALKED BUT I COULDN'T. I COULD NEVER FIND THAT PERFECT AND FINAL END TO WHAT WE WERE.

I GUESS I WASN'T THINKING BIG ENOUGH.

FUCKING AT A DIRTY CRIME SCENE.

AHHHMMM...

IS SUMMER AROUND?

SHE SAID SHE NEEDED SOMETHING PLANTED.

SHUT YOUR MOUTH AND DO ME THE FAVOUR OF DYING SILENTLY.

SUMMER PANICKED. SHE FLED. AS SUCH, SHE'S UNPREPARED BUT THE PLAN IS SIMPLE. WHAT COULD GO WRONG?

ONE NIGHT OF COMPLICATIONS DELIVERS HER INTO AN UNCOMPLICATED LIFE.

IF SHE TAKES A BOAT, SHE'LL BE HEARD AND TRACKED. THE STEALTH AND INCOGNITO OF A SLOW PADDLE IS HER GETAWAY.

THE SHARKS WERE RECENTLY FED AND SHE'S PRETTY SURE THEY'RE ASLEEP.

SUMMER IS GOING TO BE UP ALL NIGHT.

"I CAN'T SLEEP."

I...DON'T WANT TO.

HEY, IT'S OKAY, WE CAN TRY AGAIN.

IT'S OUR FIRST GO, AND I'M RIGHT HERE WITH YOU.

"WE CAN WORK IT OUT."

STOP SHOOTING AT ME!

NO.

NO.

SUMMER FINALLY GOT WHAT SHE WANTED.

SUMMER ALMOST HAD IT ALL.

AS USUAL, THE ISLAND RUINS EVERYTHING.

OR MAYBE IT'S HER...

PKOOTH.

HANNAH BALAZ WAS SITTING ON THE STORY OF THE YEAR.

ALL OF THEM.

SUMMER AND STANDARD WERE GONE. VANISHED. THERE WERE A DOZEN WAYS TO EXPLAIN THIS.

HELL OF A HEADLINE, HANNAH, YOU GOT A STORY TO MATCH IT?

...

EVERYONE'S WAITING FOR THE INSIDE SCOOP. THIS IS *YOUR* STORY.

IS IT? IT FEELS LARGER. LIKE IT'S ABOUT SOMETHING ELSE, SOMETHING MORE.

WELL, WHILE YOU HUNT THE HORIZON, CAN YOU GET DOWN TO THE WATER?

SOME DEAD SHARKS WASHED UP.

YOU CAN FIND ANOTHER STORY THERE.

AND IF YOU FOUND IT BY PRINT DEADLINE, THAT'D BE SUPER.

HANNAH FINALLY SEES THE LINKS.

THERE ARE A DOZEN WAYS TO TELL THIS STORY...

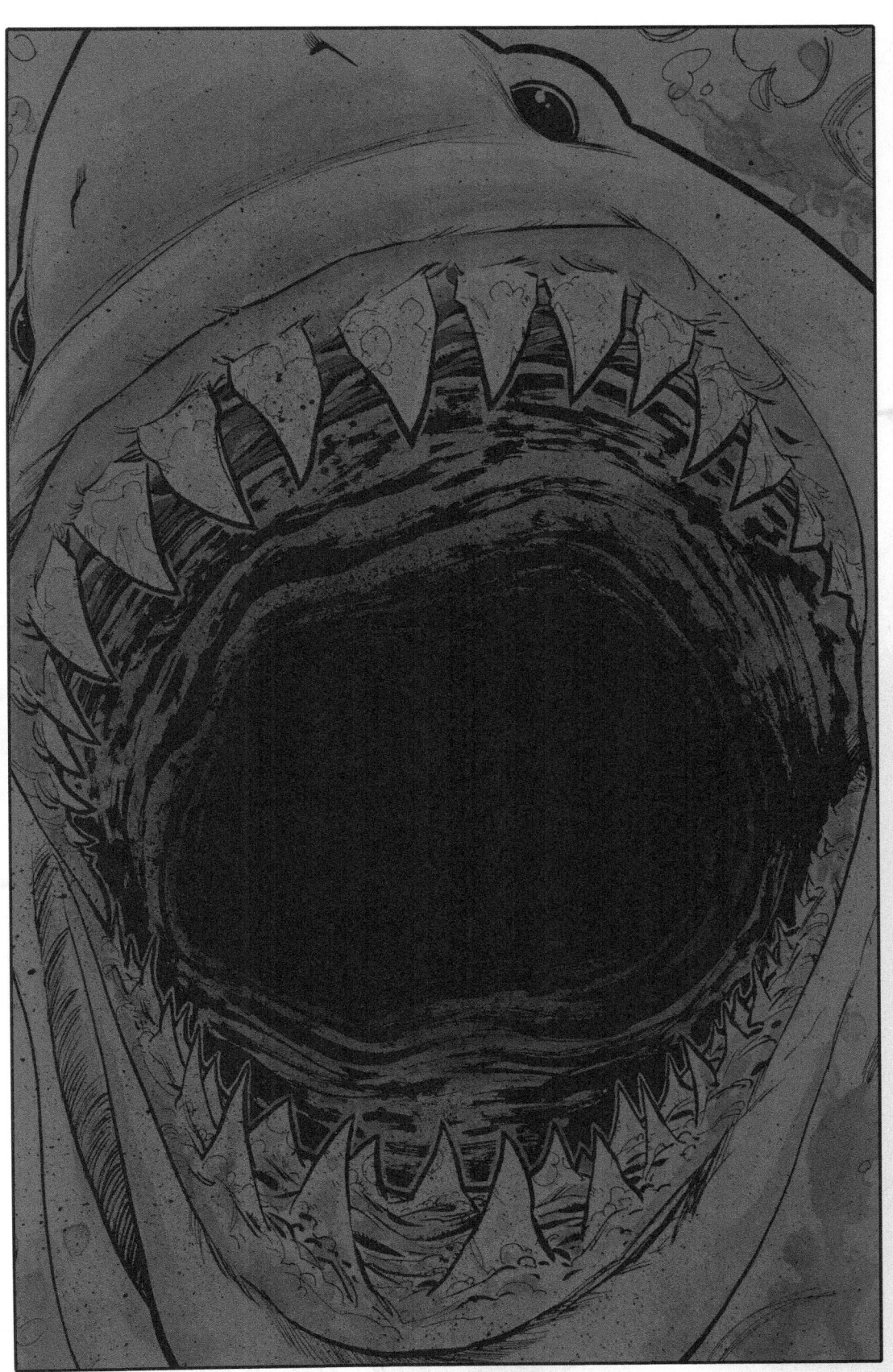

GET IN THE FUCKING SEA.

This was supposed to feel like a pulp paperback. You know the ones, they often had Gold Medals in the top corners of the covers, they were full of purple prose, and purple bruises, and you typed them on old Underwoods so they'd flip along at a mighty pace.

But this is no paperback. And that's because of Sami Kivela and Mark Dale. The bastards.

When you start getting art in that looks more beautiful than your bottle of rum held aloft to the light of the setting sun, you realise this isn't about the words, this is about the story.

Sami and Mark tell more with the inflected light tone of the ocean than I ever could with a thesaurus and five drafts. This book is gorgeous, and that's why I loved making every single page of it. Writing a surf noir comic is one thing, but to watch a surf noir comic come together is a life event. This book is a pure collaboration, and a typewritten manuscript with just one illo on the front, beautiful as it would have been, could never be enough or come close to what these gentlemen lay on the page.

CHUM aims to lure your heart out of your eyes so we might blind you while we crush your spirit.

I have to tip my hat to Sami, Mark, and Nic J Shaw for his letters, and the forever sublime edits from Dan Hill, as well as the guidance and trust shown from 'The Boss', Tyler James. This comic exists because the team at Kingsford Island HQ hustled and loved and did their very best.

Now, I hope you are holding on with two hands because this comic came to fight, and much like the characters inside, it won't quit until it's down, and has probably taken others with it.

The surf noir downward spiral, there's a long way to sink.

Ryan K Lindsay
150 km from a beach
October 2016

SIX WORD SURF NOIR STORIES

"Stolen hearts lead to salty graves."
– Ryan K Lindsay [hack]

"Shifting sands foiled the perfect getaway."
– Ricardo Mo [COLOSSI, PROPELLER]

"Both Anna and the cocaine vanished."
– Ed Brisson [THE VIOLENT, SHELTERED]

"Kicking sand castles, wet with blood."
– Christopher Sebela [HIGH CRIMES, WE(L)COME BACK]

"Too many bullets to be sharkfood."
– Danny Djeljosevic [BIG FUCKING HAMMER]

"Buried Brian Wilson. God only knows."
– Duane Swierczynski [THE IMMORTAL IRON FIST, THE BLACK HOOD]

"Crimson sand beneath his broken nails."
– James Maddox [CLOWN, THE DEAD]

"His tan disappeared after the girl."
– Chris Lewis [KARMA POLICE, DRONES]

"My breath sank, his body floated."
– Nic J Shaw [THE FIX, IMAGINARY DRUGS]

"Rolling tides scrubbed the bloodstained beach."
– Jeremy Holt [SOUTHERN DOG, SKIP TO THE END]

"Tendrils of seaweed and of leviathans."
– Shaun Manning [INTERESTING DRUG, MACBETH: THE RED KING]

"The riptide carried her home, forever."
– Jason Ciaramella [JOE HILL'S THE CAPE, C IS FOR CTHULHU]

"Red sun, red hands, red lights."
– Forrest C. Helvie [THE ADVENTURES OF WHIZ BANG: THE BOY ROBOT]

"Spindrift kissed the beachcomber's body bye-bye."
– Cameron Ashley [CRIME FACTORY]

"She sank fast, like his heart."
– Sierra Dean [SOMETHING SECRET THIS WAY COMES, A BLOODY GOOD]

"A human tooth embedded in driftwood."
– Alex Paknadel [TURNCOAT, ARCADIA]

"Children can only swim so long."
– James Burton II [INHERITANCE, DAMAGE INC.]

"The tide was always his accomplice."
– Dan Hill [DISCONNECT]

"Neck deep in debt...now sand."
– Ryan Ferrier [TIGER LAWYER, KENNEL BLOCK BLUES]

"She sold sea shells. Not anymore."
– Tom Taylor [BATMAN/SUPERMAN, ALL NEW WOLVERINE]

RYAN K LINDSAY - WRITER

A man of many worlds, Ryan K Lindsay writes comics, about comics, and teaches comics. His credits include NEGATIVE SPACE from Dark Horse Comics, HEADSPACE from Monkeybrain Comics/IDW, GLOVES a short story in the Vertigo CMYK anthology, and the Kickstarter runaway success DEER EDITOR from his 'Four Colour Ray Gun' imprint. He was also tapped to join the DC Writers Workshop Talent Development group in 2016. He's written/edited analytical texts, including THE DEVIL IS IN THE DETAILS: EXAMINING MATT MURDOCK AND DAREDEVIL from Sequart, and NOIRVEMBER and YMMV through 'Four Colour Ray Gun'. He has had essays published in Criminal, Godzilla, Sheltered, Strange Nation, and Crime Factory. He is Australian.

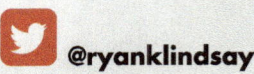 @ryanklindsay

SAMI KIVELA - ARTIST

Sami Kivela is a comic book artist, whose credits include GRIMM FAIRY TALES PRESENTS: REALM WAR, HIT LIST, GRIMM TALES OF TERROR Vol. 2 #10, and INFERNO AGE OF DARKNESS from Zenescope, DARK LIES, DARKER TRUTHS (GN) from Markosia, and THE HEAP from Moonstone Books. He's also the artist and co-creator of the antler noir series DEER EDITOR. He has had short stories published by Ape Entertainment, Egmont, and Heske Horror, among others. In addition to producing sequential art, he has illustrated and designed numerous comic book and album covers. Sami lives and works in his native Finland, far away from sharks.

 @sami_kivela

MARK DALE - COLORIST

Mark Dale has been colouring comics for the past 2 years, getting his start by producing 5 fill in pages for TUROK: THE DINOSAUR HUNTER #5 by Dynamite Entertainment. Since then he's worked on several self-published comic series that have been sold at conventions in the US and worldwide and is working on several exciting projects that will be coming soon. Mark works and lives in the UK.

 @pleurgh

NIC J SHAW - LETTERER

Nic J Shaw is a comic book letterer and graphic designer. He believes in love at first site, that coffee isn't just for closers, and that the earth is probably flat. Nic has worked with Image Comics, IDW, Dark Horse, and Black Mask. You can find him dodging land-sharks and wallabies in Sydney, Australia.

 @Ironbark_